KT-557-228

Looking for Billie

by

Rosie Rushton

Illustrated by Karen Donnelly

You do not need to read this page - just get on with the book!

First published in 2004 in Great Britain by
Barrington Stoke Ltd, Sandeman House, Trunk's Close,
55 High Street, Edinburgh EH1 1SR

Copyright © 2004 Rosie Rushton
Illustrations © Karen Donnelly

The moral right of the author has been asserted in
accordance with the Copyright, Designs and
Patents Act 1988

ISBN 1-842992-06-6

Printed in Great Britain by Bell & Bain Ltd

MEET THE AUTHOR – ROSIE RUSHTON

What is your favourite animal?
The horse
What is your favourite boy's name?
Alexander – my grandson's name
What is your favourite girl's name?
Nicola, Sally, Caroline – the
names of my terrific daughters
What is your favourite food?
Fish with roasted vegetables
What is your favourite music?
Classical, choral, Celine Dion
What is your favourite hobby?
Reading and country walks

MEET THE ILLUSTRATOR – KAREN DONNELLY

What is your favourite animal?
Woodlice!
What is your favourite boy's name?
Laurie
What is your favourite girl's name?
Jean
What is your favourite food?
Sausages and runny eggs
What is your favourite music?
Beck
What is your favourite hobby?
Drawing and printmaking

To Ruth Archer

Contents

Chapter 1
How it all began ...

When I was a little kid, I was good. In fact, I was so good that people kept talking about it.

"Billie's such a good girl," Wendy used to say. Wendy is my foster mum.

"As good as gold," Steve, my foster dad, always added, waiting to make sure everyone got the joke. "Gold – get it?"

My last name is Gold – Billie Gold.
At least, that's what everyone calls me.
No one knows what my real surname is.

But then, no one knows much about me
at all. Even I don't know much about me.

What I do know is that when I left Hull
Street Primary and went to Benton
Comprehensive, people stopped saying I
was good.

"Billie's changed," Wendy said with a
sigh at least once a week.

Of course I'd changed. Being a teacher's
pet doesn't make you popular at Benton.

"Billie's turning into a typical teenager,"
Steve would say every time anyone asked
about me.

He was wrong of course. I may be 13 –
but typical? I don't think so.

"Billie's work is late, messy and not up to her usual standard," my form tutor moaned at parents' evening. That was because I had more important things to worry about than the First World War, volcanoes or French verbs.

"Since she changed schools, Billie doesn't care about anything any more," Wendy would say every Sunday when she phoned her mother.

That's where she was wrong. There was one thing I cared about more than anything else in the world. I daydreamed about it in class. I stared at myself in the mirror looking for clues. I even thought about writing to the newspapers to ask for help.

But I never did a thing about it. Not until we had our class trip to London.

And I saw her. The woman I had dreamed of finding.

The woman on the train. The woman I thought could be – no, had to be – my mum.

****

I guess I had better start at the beginning. I was found in a carrier bag outside the police station when I was about three days old. It wasn't any old carrier bag. It was a bright pink one with proper handles. It came from one of those posh shops in the High Street, where the sales girls sniff if you go in with muddy trainers. I was wrapped in a blue blanket and there was a funny little woolly lamb tucked in beside me. I've still got the lamb. All the stuffing has fallen out and an ear's missing, but I still keep it under my pillow.

There's something else I keep. It's a torn scrap of paper that the policeman found at the bottom of the carrier bag. It just says:

Please look after Billie until ...

That's all. But you see, it's really important. It's the word "until" that matters. I'm pretty sure it must have said "Please look after Billie until I come back to get her". And then there would have been the name of the person writing it. Something like "Love, Jane", or "Best wishes, Sharon". I wish it hadn't been torn. At least that way I'd have known the name of my mum. Or my dad. Or someone.

Don't get me wrong – I love Wendy and Steve. They're the nicest foster parents I've ever had. But they are not my real family. I don't belong to them – I'm just there because someone has to look after me and they get paid to do it. And the older I got,

the more that bothered me. I started to feel as if I didn't know who I really was.

"You don't look like your mum, do you?" people said to me when I started my new school. It's true. Wendy and Steve are short and dumpy, and I'm tall and skinny. I've got bright red hair that won't lie flat, and their hair is mousy brown. Well, Wendy's is. Steve hasn't got much hair at all.

And that's not all. Wendy is really good at art, and I can't even hold a paintbrush. Steve's mad about sport, and I'll do anything to get out of P.E. and games. Wendy's got a Welsh accent, Steve's from Glasgow. And me? Who knows? I could be anyone. Or nobody.

Most days, it feels like I'm nobody.

Whenever people asked questions, I told them I was fostered. But I never told anyone about being found in a bag. I never told them that the reason my surname is Gold is because that was the name of the children's ward in the hospital where the police took me when they found me.

I just pretended that my parents had died.

I spent most of my 13th birthday wondering whether my real mother was thinking about me, wishing she hadn't dumped me and thinking about all the presents she would be buying me if only she knew where I was. I even wondered whether the 11th of November was my real birthday, or just a date that the doctors had guessed at.

"Billie, what's on your mind?" Wendy asked me, because she's a really kind person. "If you've got a problem, we're here to help. But you have to tell us what it is."

I didn't want to upset her, or make her think I didn't like her, so I just said I wasn't feeling well. I said that my stomach hurt and so did my head. She said it must be hormones and that I'd be starting my periods any day now. About time, too. There were only three people left in my class who hadn't started and it was dead embarrassing. If they didn't come soon, I'd have to pretend.

"I expect starting late runs in your family," Lisa told me. "Not that you'll ever know."

Lisa's the only one of my mates who knows about the carrier bag bit of my life. I never meant to tell her. It just came out one day when she was crying because her dad had left home to live with Bimbo Bev and her mum kept taking tablets for her nerves and forgetting to buy supper.

"You're so lucky having a mum and dad who care about you," she sniffed.

So I told her that Wendy and Steve weren't my real parents and that I hadn't a clue where I came from. Just to make her feel better about her life.

"That is so romantic!" she breathed. "Just think about it. You could be the love child of someone dead famous."

Lisa has a very vivid imagination. She's always making up stories, and she can lie her way out of detention better than anyone I know. Lisa is the sort of person who always manages to do exactly what she wants. Except control her parents, that is.

That's why I'm glad I told her. That's why I'm glad it was Lisa who was with me that day.

The day that people began to see that I was not always as good as gold.

Chapter 2
What did you say?

If Lisa hadn't been hungry on the train, I would never have seen the woman.

"We need to get crisps and chocolate," she insisted. "Listening to Miss Webber going on about moons and planets and stuff at the Science Museum is going to be bad enough, without having to do it on an empty stomach."

Miss Webber is our science teacher. She was meant to book a coach to take us to London but she forgot. We thought we'd miss out on the trip, but she and Mr Brown (who teaches P.E. and is madly in love with Miss Webber) decided to take us by train. There were only 16 of us on the trip and I guess they thought they could cope. I think after what happened, they wished they'd stayed in school.

Anyway, when we got to the buffet car, we saw this really huge woman leaning on the counter with a big pile of rolls and sandwiches and pastries in front of her. She was dressed from head to foot in purple velvet and every time she moved to pick up a sandwich, her boobs bounced up and down and a dozen gold bangles jangled on her wrists. On her head she wore a turban, held in place with an enormous green butterfly brooch. She looked like someone out of Aladdin.

"Now tell me, dear," she said to the girl working in the train buffet, "does this roll have butter in it? Because I don't touch butter. It does? Oh dear."

She tossed it aside.

"And this doughnut – is it sugar free?" she demanded.

Well, I ask you. Have you ever seen a sugar-free doughnut?

She went on for ages, prodding every sandwich with long scarlet fingernails, and trying to sniff the contents through the wrappers.

"I've decided!" the woman declared in the end. "I'll just have ..."

She stopped in mid-sentence because her mobile phone went off – loudly. Grabbing it from her huge handbag, she clamped it to her ear.

"Hello? Pixie here – who's that?"

"Pixie?" Lisa spluttered. "What kind of a name is that?"

The sales girl grinned, raised her eyebrows and leaned towards us across the counter.

"Can I get you something?" she asked. "Don't worry about her, she'll take forever. She's the same every day."

"I'll have a Mars Bar and a Twix and a Kit Kat Chunky …" Lisa began.

She had just finished listing all the chocolate bars you could think of when the loudspeaker crackled.

"We shall shortly be arriving at London St Pancras where this train terminates. Please ensure you take all your personal belongings with you."

"Oh my goodness!" The woman called Pixie swung round, elbowed Lisa out of the way and grabbed a flapjack. She slammed a pound coin on to the counter.

"Got to go," she shouted into the phone. "We're at the station."

She pushed past us, heading for the door.

"Ouch!" Lisa squealed as one of Pixie's high-heeled boots landed on her toe. Pixie was far too busy shouting into her phone to notice.

"What am I doing?" she boomed into the phone. "What do you think I'm doing, you stupid man?"

She sighed crossly.

"I'm doing what I've been doing for the past three years. Looking for Billie."

****

I put those little stars at the end of that bit of my story because I can't quite remember what happened next. I remember my knees turning to jelly. I remember staring at Pixie as she grappled with the door handle and stepped onto the platform. I remember Miss Webber yelling at Lisa and me for hanging about at the buffet and not staying with our group.

And I remember Lisa grabbing my arm as Pixie hitched her bag over her shoulder and strode off down the platform, her heels clicking on the stone floor.

"Billie!" Lisa cried. "Did you hear what she said?"

I nodded. My mouth had gone dry and I seemed to have lost the power of speech.

"Well, don't just stand there!" Lisa shouted. "Go after her."

"I can't," I blurted out. "I mean, what would I say?"

"Tell her you're Billie, of course," Lisa replied. "She said she was looking for Billie. Don't you see? She could be your mum."

"She can't be," I insisted. But even as I said it, my mind began to race. What if she was? What if fate had made Miss Webber forget to book the coach? What if I was *meant* to be on that train that very morning, when Pixie was on it, too?

"Right, everyone," Miss Webber ordered, breaking into my thoughts. "I want you to walk briskly in pairs to the Underground. Mr Brown will lead the way, I'll come at the end."

Honestly, she made a simple walk along a station platform sound like an army exercise.

"Keep together now," Mr Brown cut in. "Follow me."

"Billie," Lisa hissed in my ear, as we all went through the ticket barrier, "it's now or never. Look, she's way ahead of us."

I bit my lip. Lisa was right. Any second now Pixie would vanish into the crowd and I would never see her again.

"Miss, I need the loo," I whispered, tapping Miss Webber on the arm.

"Well, you'll have to wait until we get to the museum," Miss Webber began.

"I can't, miss," I yelled, breaking into a run.

"Me neither," I heard Lisa cry behind me. "We'll meet you at the Underground."

I tried to close my ears to Miss Webber's cries of dismay and prayed that Mr Brown wouldn't follow us.

We sprinted past the barrier, ignoring the ticket collector's shouts and pounded across the station. Pixie was almost out of sight, walking quickly towards the sign marked *TAXIS*.

If Pixie hadn't walked so fast, or if the laces of my trainer hadn't come undone at that very moment, I am sure we would have caught up with her. But by the time we got to the taxi rank, she had climbed into a black cab and was slamming the door shut behind her.

"Wait!" Lisa shouted at the top of her voice, jumping up and down and waving her arms in the air.

For one wonderful moment, I thought Pixie had spotted us waving and shouting. She turned and looked at me full in the face.

Then she leaned forward, said something to the driver, and the black cab pulled away.

Just as the cab was edging its way into the stream of traffic, Pixie pulled her turban off her head and shook her hair loose.

Her hair was bright red. Not pale and wishy-washy, not rust or ginger. Flaming traffic light orange. Just like mine.

Chapter 3
Follow that cab!

"Come on, quick!" Lisa grabbed my wrist and pulled me towards the next waiting taxi cab.

"What are you doing?" I protested.

"We're going to follow her, of course," Lisa told me, pulling open the cab door. "Get in."

"You're out of your mind!" I yelled, trying to break free from her vice-like grip. "We can't just bunk off."

"Get real, Billie!" she shouted. "You'll never have another chance like this. Now get in!"

Lisa pushed me, none too gently, into the cab and slammed the door shut.

"Follow *that* black taxi!" she shouted to the taxi driver. "Quick!"

"I don't know about that," the driver began, chewing on a piece of gum.

"My mate's mother's in there," Lisa said quickly. "They've had this awful row, and my mate here wants to say sorry."

The cab driver grunted.

"That's nice," he muttered. "A kid who cares. Rare thing these days."

He pulled away from the kerb. My heart began pounding.

"Lisa, you're bonkers. Miss Webber will go ballistic – she'll be hopping mad," I whispered.

"So? What's more important, your entire future or a couple of detentions from that loser Miss Webber?"

I had to admit she had a point. It was just that I wasn't used to breaking the rules. Lisa, on the other hand, is an expert at it. If they did GCSEs in rule breaking, she'd get an A*, no problem.

"It's obvious that woman's your mum," Lisa muttered, trying not to let the taxi driver hear what she was saying. "Until I saw her, I thought you were the only person on the planet with that colour hair."

She squeezed my hand.

"Just think," she sighed, "there's your mum in a taxi looking for you and she doesn't know you're right behind her. It's like something out of a film."

The thing about films is that something bad always happens just when you don't expect it.

And that's what was about to happen to us.

****

The taxi was edging its way down a really crowded street, and we could still just about see Pixie's black cab in the far distance. Then, all at once, the intercom in our cab crackled into life.

"Oscar three seven, are you receiving?"

The cab driver flicked a switch.

"Go ahead," he said in a bored kind of voice.

"We've got some mad woman on the line in a right panic. Have you got two kids in your cab? A red head and one with a ponytail?"

I gasped. Lisa said a word, but as it was a rather bad word, I won't mention it here.

"They've run away from a school group. Teacher's in a right state. Get them to the Science Museum at once, OK."

"Run away, huh?" The driver glared at us over his left shoulder. "All that talk of mothers. You kids, you're all the same. Lying, bunking off ..."

"It's not a lie!" Lisa shouted. "That woman is my mate's mum, OK?"

"Oh sure," the guy retorted. "And I'm Spiderman."

"Please," Lisa begged. "You have to believe us. We have to catch up with her. Billie's whole future is on the line here."

"My job will be on the line if I don't get you two back to your teacher," he spat, turning off his intercom and speeding up round a corner.

"You can't do this to us!" Lisa yelled at him.

"Watch me," he grunted.

"I told you it was a crazy idea," I snapped at Lisa, trying hard not to cry. "We are going to be in dead trouble and for what? Some woman I'm never going to see again."

"That's where you're wrong," Lisa retorted.

"Wrong about getting a real roasting from Miss Webber? I don't think so," I answered.

"No, silly," she said. "You're wrong about never seeing that Pixie woman again. I'm not the sort of person who gives up easily. We'll find her, whatever it takes. Get it?"

I didn't get it. Frankly, I thought she was talking a load of rubbish. But I didn't have time to tell her that because the taxi was pulling up outside the entrance to the Science Museum. And striding up and down the pavement with a face like thunder was Mr Brown.

Chapter 4
Teacher Trouble

"And what do you two have to say for yourselves?" Mr Brown thundered as we opened the taxi door.

"Sorry, sir," I mumbled.

"Sorry? Is that all? Pay the driver at once and then I shall deal with you both."

Lisa and I glanced at one another.

"How much?" I muttered to the driver.

"Nine pounds," he said.

"Nine pounds!" Lisa screeched. "That's a total rip-off!"

Mr Brown's face turned a livid shade of purple.

"Lisa Jenkins," he stormed, "how dare you be so rude!"

"But, sir, I've only got five pounds," she stammered.

"Me too," I nodded. "It will take all my spending money."

"You should have thought about that before running off," he shouted, as we handed over all our cash to the grumpy-looking driver.

"You have caused a lot of trouble for a great many people," Mr Brown said, marching us into the museum. "How could you have been so stupid?"

"I thought I saw someone I knew," I burst out. "Someone I hadn't seen for ages."

I thought that might get him off our backs, but of course, it just made him even more cross.

"Well, fancy that," he said, with a sarcastic smile. "So if Miss Webber and I had spotted an old friend in the distance, do you think we would have dashed off and left you all stranded?"

"I wish you had," Lisa muttered.

"I beg your pardon?" Mr Brown asked, his bushy eyebrows meeting in an angry frown.

"No, sir," we chanted together. "Sorry, sir."

I didn't get a chance to talk to Lisa for the rest of the day. Miss Webber made Lisa go in her group, and sent me off with Mr Brown. I got the worst part of the deal. Mr Brown only smiles twice a year and his smelly armpits are a danger to health and safety. I had to spend the whole day filling in stupid worksheets and watching videos about the night sky. And all the time, I was thinking about Pixie.

And her red hair.

And the fact that she was, right then, somewhere in London looking for Billie.

And that just maybe, the Billie she was looking for was me.

****

Chapter 5
Making Plans

"I can't believe that we were so close to finding your mum," Lisa sighed for the tenth time as we walked home from the station at teatime.

"Don't keep going on about it," I snapped, kicking an empty cola can into the gutter. "We didn't find her and that's an end to it. Just forget it, will you?"

I knew I couldn't forget it, but at that moment something else was on my mind.

"Did you hear what Miss Webber said on the way home?" I asked Lisa. "She's going to report us to the Head. He's sure to ring Wendy and Steve and I'll be in real trouble."

"So? You get grounded for a few days – what's the big deal?" Lisa replied. "Get a life, Billie!"

I didn't like to tell her that I'd never been grounded before. Ticked off, made to do the washing-up every night for a week, yes. But grounded and not allowed out with my mates? Never.

"I've got it!" Lisa cried suddenly, stopping dead in her tracks and grabbing my arm. "Why didn't I think of it before? It's simple."

"What is?" I muttered.

"We get the train again tomorrow, right? That way we can sit next to her and you can tell her who you are."

"Lisa, what are you on about?" I said. "That's the dumbest idea I've ever heard."

"Why?" Lisa snapped.

"Just because Pixie was on the train today, doesn't mean she'll be on it tomorrow, stupid," I stressed.

"That's where you're wrong," Lisa said, with a grin. "Remember what the girl at the buffet said? She said she took forever to choose her food *every day.*"

"Every day!" I repeated. My mind was racing. "You're right."

For a moment, my heart lifted. It soon sank again.

"We can't just skip school and catch a train," I argued.

"Billie Gold, which is more important?" Lisa retorted. "One day of school, or your whole future?"

Put like that, there was only one answer.

"My future," I whispered, my heart beginning to thump in my chest.

"Right!" Lisa grinned. "Now, listen carefully. This is what you have to do."

****

I couldn't sleep that night. I am not sure whether it was excitement or guilt that kept me awake. I was excited at the thought that, just possibly, I might meet Pixie the next day, but very guilty because of what I had done after supper.

I thought I would get found out, most of all when Steve grumbled that his running partner hadn't phoned him to arrange where to meet. Well, he couldn't, could he? I had unplugged every phone in the house. Like Lisa said, we couldn't have the Head ringing up to make a fuss and putting the parents on Red Alert. Not yet.

That was the easy bit. Taking the money was a lot harder. I've got some cash in the bank but there was no time to get that, so I had to take it from Wendy's bag. I felt sick doing it. I put it back three times.

But then I said to myself that it was only a loan. When I'd found Pixie, and told Steve and Wendy the whole story, they would understand.

All I had to do was to find Pixie and then everything would come right.

You wouldn't think a person could get to be 13 years old and still be so dumb, would you?

Chapter 6
Second-class Citizens

"Have you switched your mobile off?" Lisa asked as we waited for the train to leave Bedford Station.

"No, why should I?" I asked.

"Use your brain," Lisa replied. "When the school phones home to say we haven't arrived, Wendy will phone you, right?"

My stomach turned over.

"I hadn't thought of that," I admitted, punching the OFF button on my phone.

"Which is why you've got me to sort you out," Lisa teased. "Hey, we're moving! Come on!"

We ran through the coaches until we reached the buffet car.

There was no sign of Pixie. But the same girl as before was wiping crumbs from the counter.

"You know the woman who was here yesterday?" Lisa panted. "Has she been here today?"

The girl stared at her. She looked bored.

"What woman? We get hundreds of women coming here," she said.

"The one with the turban," Lisa insisted. "The fussy one."

"Oh, her!" the girl grinned. "Pixie Petruso."

"Hey, Billie," Lisa whispered, nudging me in the ribs, "sounds like you're Italian."

I had to think about that. I wasn't at all sure I wanted to be Italian. I don't even like pasta.

"What did you say?" The girl leaned across the counter and frowned.

"I just said that Petruso sounded like an Italian name," Lisa replied quickly.

"Well, of course it is – everyone knows that," the girl said, turning to serve a tall guy in a smart suit. "Don't you watch telly? She was in that Friday night play last week

– the one about the gipsy woman who finds out she's a princess."

She turned away from us then, and started fluttering her eyelashes at the tall guy and giggling.

"TV?" Lisa gasped. "I knew it! She's famous."

She tapped her foot as she waited for the man to march off with his prawn sandwich and paper cup of coffee.

"So where is she?" she demanded. "You said she got the train every day."

"She does," the girl nodded. "She gets on at Kettering."

"Ace!" Lisa turned round and slapped my hand. "We've cracked it."

"You won't get to talk to her," the girl warned, eyeing us up and down. "She hates to be bothered. That's why she travels first class."

"Where's that?" I asked.

"Front two coaches," the girl said.

"Thanks!" We grinned at one another and began pushing our way towards the front of the train, ignoring the girl's shouts of protest.

"And just where do you two think you are going?" The ticket inspector blocked the doorway to the first-class coaches.

"We've got to see Pixie Petruso," Lisa began. "We've got something that belongs to her."

The ticket inspector shook his head and laughed.

"Not that old story again," he sighed. "Can't you think of a better one?"

He pulled the door shut behind him.

"Now get back to your seats," he ordered. "Unless of course, you want to pay an extra 25 pounds to travel first class."

"But we have to see ..."

"What you have to do, miss," he retorted, "is push off. Leave Miss Petruso alone. She's paid for a bit of privacy. She doesn't want to be bothered by anyone."

We had no choice, particularly as he followed us all the way back to our seats and then stood watching us as though we were a couple of convicts on the run.

"We'll just have to catch her when the train gets to London," Lisa said. "It's so exciting. She must be famous. And I expect she's very rich, too."

She looked at me with envy.

"Promise me something," she said, touching my arm.

"What?"

"When you're living in some posh house with Pixie, remember it was me that made it all happen, OK?"

"Sure," I nodded.

"You could look a bit happier about it," she protested.

The funny thing was, I didn't feel very happy. I felt scared. I hadn't really thought about what would happen if I found my real mum. Would I have to move somewhere else? Leave Wendy and Steve? I hadn't thought about any of that.

And why should I move, even if she did turn out to be my mum? Where was she when I needed her? Did she dump me because a baby would spoil her lifestyle?

If Lisa was right, and Pixie had loads of cash, why couldn't she have found me and sent me some? Remembered my birthdays? Been a proper mother?

By the time the train reached London, I wasn't just nervous. I was angry.

Very angry indeed.

Chapter 7

It wasn't meant to be like this ...

We jumped off the train, ran down the platform and saw Pixie as she was going through the ticket gate. This time she was wearing a bright pink, fur-trimmed coat and a black turban with a huge fake flower on the top.

If she did turn out to be my mum, I'd have to get her sorted and do something about her dress sense.

We sprinted as fast as we could and caught up with her at the taxi rank.

"Excuse me, we have to talk to you!" Lisa leapt in front of her, blocking her path as she made for the first free cab.

"Not now, dears," Pixie replied. A cloud of perfume wafted towards us. She raised her hand and waved down a taxi. "I'm in a hurry."

She pulled open the door of the cab.

"No! Wait!" I was panting so hard that the words almost stuck in my throat. "It's really important."

"I'm sorry but I've no time for autographs now," she replied, hardly looking at me. She climbed into the cab and began shutting the door.

"Please, listen," Lisa shouted, grabbing the door handle. "We don't want an autograph."

"You don't?" Pixie looked almost offended.

"No," Lisa went on. "We know what you're doing – looking for Billie, right?"

"Yes, dear, too right," Pixie replied. "Sometimes I think I'll be doing it for the rest of my life. Day after day, looking for Billie."

She tried to pull the door closed, but Lisa was holding onto it for dear life.

"Child, let go of that door!"

Suddenly, Pixie's voice was harsh as she spat out the words.

"No, I won't!" Lisa shouted. "Just listen, will you? You don't have to do it any more."

"What *are* you talking about?" By now, Pixie was looking really angry.

"You don't have to look any more. Here she is," Lisa told her, with passion. "Your daughter."

"My daughter?" Her face went white and she clamped a hand to her mouth.

"Yes, me," I smiled. "I'm Billie."

"How dare you say such a thing!" Pixie exploded. "There is no possible way that you are my daughter!"

And that's when I went mad.

"Oh, so you don't like the look of me, is that it? Decided that you won't claim me after all?"

I gulped back the tears.

"I suppose you'd like to pretend I never existed, is that it?" I blurted out.

Pixie's face was turning a horrid shade of purple.

"Excuse me," the driver butted in, "but are we going somewhere or not? There's a queue behind us, you know."

"Yes, we're going right now," Pixie said, finally getting the door away from Lisa and slamming it shut. "Papa Gino's restaurant, Covent Garden – and fast!"

"You can't just go!" Lisa shouted through the window. "You can't just dump your daughter."

"Oh, yes she can!" By now I was sobbing. "She's done it before."

Pixie didn't reply. But as the taxi drove away, I saw her drop her head into her hands. Her shoulders began shaking.

"How *dare* she laugh at me!" I spluttered through my tears.

Lisa touched my arm.

"She's not laughing, Billie," she said softly. "She's crying."

"Crying?" I whispered.

Lisa nodded.

"That's the final proof," she said. "She *is* your mum. She's crying because she's so upset she feels so guilty about you."

****

Chapter 8
The end of the dream?

There was no way we could afford a taxi so we had to catch an Underground train. It took ages and as we got closer to Covent Garden, I started to feel more and more nervous.

"This is stupid," I muttered to Lisa over and over again. "She doesn't want to know. If she had, she wouldn't have driven off."

"That was the shock," Lisa said knowingly. "I've read about it in magazines. People act funny and then wish they hadn't. We're just giving her a second chance, that's all."

It wasn't difficult to spot Pixie when we found our way to Papa Gino's restaurant. She was the sort of person who stood out in a crowd. She was sitting at a corner table, sipping a glass of wine and chatting to a tall guy with floppy black hair.

"What now?" I asked Lisa. "We can't just march up to them."

"Watch me," Lisa replied, grabbing my hand.

She dragged me over to the table.

"Remember us?" she said.

"The girls from the station," she exclaimed. "I'm sorry – I must have seemed very rude."

"It's OK," I began, a bit surprised to hear her say sorry.

"No, it's not OK!" Lisa cut in, glaring at Pixie. "How could you do that?"

"Do what?" Pixie asked, looking puzzled.

"Drive off like that," Lisa told her. "Just when we'd found you."

"Look, dear," Pixie sighed. "I can't talk to you right now. This young man is here to interview me for a newspaper."

"Oh, well, that's good," Lisa said airily, turning to the guy who was watching us with his mouth half open, "because this is an ace story."

"It is?" the guy mumbled.

"Sure," Lisa said with a broad grin. "This is Billie. She's Pixie's long-lost daughter."

"Really?" The guy looked excited. "Pixie, is this true?"

Pixie didn't answer. She just stared at me.

"Billie?" Pixie murmured. "Your name is Billie?"

I nodded eagerly. She had to accept me now – I've never met another girl called Billie in my whole life.

"Pixie – is this true?" the reporter repeated, scribbling away on his notepad.

"Of course it's not true, you stupid boy!" Pixie exploded. "These children have just come up with some wild story."

"We're not children and it's not a story," I burst out in panic. "You've been looking for me. Well, here I am."

Pixie stared at me.

"But I haven't been looking for anyone," she began.

I felt myself getting angry all over again.

"Yes, you have," I insisted. "We heard what you said on the train."

Pixie was staring at me, shaking her head. Then, all at once, her eyes grew large and she put her hand over her mouth.

"Just what was it that you heard me saying?" she asked, gazing at me.

"You said you were looking for Billie," I repeated. I wondered if I really wanted a mother who was so thick. "Yesterday, when you were talking on the phone."

"Oh." Pixie closed her eyes. Her eyelids were covered with bright green eyeshadow. "Looking for Billie. So that's it."

She gave a faint smile.

"Yes, that's it," Lisa went on. "And this is Billie, the baby you dumped in a carrier bag."

"A carrier bag?" the reporter cried. He sounded thrilled with the idea.

"You were left in a bag?" Pixie gasped. "Oh, you poor child!"

She picked up her glass and took a swig of wine.

"Look, let me just finish this interview, and then I'll show you something that will sort out this silly mistake once and for all."

I shouldn't have done what I did next. I didn't mean to. It just happened.

"Is that what you thought I was when I was born?" I heard myself say. "A silly mistake?"

"My dear girl," she began, but I didn't let her speak.

"I guess you thought you'd got rid of me for ever, didn't you? I guess being rich and famous mattered more than keeping your baby."

By now I was really sobbing. Lisa fished in her pocket and pushed a grubby tissue into my hand. The reporter went on scribbling as if his life depended on it.

"If you knew," Pixie burst out. "If you only knew! If I'd had a baby ..."

She snatched off her turban, flung it to one side and buried her face in her hands.

As the turban fell to the floor, I gasped.

Lisa gasped.

Pixie's hair was cropped close to her head.

And it was jet black.

"Your hair!" I stammered. "It's not red."

"Of course it's not red," she snapped.

She paused, staring at my tangled curls.

"Oh," she said. "I get it. You saw me yesterday, didn't you? Wearing my wig?"

"Your wig?" My heart sank even further. I could see now that she didn't look at all like me. Without the red hair, she could be just anybody.

"I was trying to get used to the wretched thing," she said wearily. "I've got to wear it for an advert for frozen pizza."

She stood up and flung on her coat.

"I'll be back in a moment," she called.

"Where are you going?" I asked. Not that I cared. She didn't matter to me any more.

"Wait two minutes, and you'll find out," she said, striding towards the door. "Follow me."

We followed her down the road and turned a corner.

"Look," she said, pointing to the theatre across the road.

And that's when I understood.

In huge lights, across the top of the theatre, were the words:

LOOKING FOR BILLIE

A play in three acts

starring

PIXIE PETRUSO and MAX GRAY

"Oh no!" Lisa gasped.

The letters on the theatre blurred as my eyes filled with tears again.

"It's a play," I said dully. "And you're not my mum."

"I am so sorry," Pixie said gently. "I would have loved nothing better than to have a daughter like you. I did have one, once."

She pressed her lips together and closed her eyes for a second.

"She died when she was a few hours old."

To my horror, two tears shone on her long mascara-laden eyelashes and then rolled slowly down her cheeks.

I had a huge lump in my throat.

"I'm sorry," I whispered. "I didn't mean to shout at you. I just wanted to know where I came from, that's all."

I gulped.

"We'll go then," I muttered.

"No, wait!" Pixie took my arm. "Look, tell me where you live. I'd like to send you tickets to see the play."

"I'm not supposed to give my address to strangers," I told her.

"Very sensible, too," Pixie nodded. "Give me your school address and I'll send them to the head teacher. What's his name?" She fished a piece of paper out of her handbag.

"Mr Carter, Benton Comprehensive School, Bedford," I told her.

"Right," Pixie said, flipping her pen back into her bag. "I suppose today's a day off, then?"

All at once, Lisa went pale. "What's the time?"

"1.30," Pixie said. "Why?"

"Got to go," I gasped. "We have to get back home before we're found out."

Pixie's eyes widened.

"You don't mean to say that you bunked off school to find me?" she asked.

I nodded.

"Right," she said briskly. She waved to a passing taxi. "I'll pay for you to get back to the station."

She opened the cab door.

"One more thing, Billie."

"Yes?"

"Don't worry about where you came from, my dear," she smiled. "It's where you're going that matters."

What she didn't know was that right then I was heading straight into very deep trouble.

Chapter 9
Leave it to Lisa

"Check your phone," Lisa ordered, as the train pulled out of the station. "That way, we will know if we've been missed."

I punched the ON button.

7 messages

The words flashed up on the screen.

Where are you? Ring me at once. Wendy.

That was the first text.

Very worried. Please ring. Wendy.

The second text.

Each text got more frantic.

The last one was the worst.

We are calling the police. Please let us know you are safe, darling. You are not in trouble. Wendy.

I burst into tears. "She's calling the police," I gasped. Lisa's face turned pale.

"Ring her now," she ordered. "Tell her we're OK. Quick."

"But where shall I say we are?" I stammered. "What shall I say we've been doing?"

"Oh, give me the phone!" Lisa said crossly. She grabbed my mobile and punched in some numbers.

"Hi, is that Wendy? It's Lisa here."

She paused.

"We're on a train from London. Yes, we're fine. We'll be home in about an hour. Pardon?"

She winked at me and put her finger to her lips.

"Sorry, bad signal. You're breaking up. See you soon. Bye!"

She chucked the phone into my lap and grinned.

"Try again," I said. "The signal might have come back."

"You are dumb," she retorted. "I never lost the signal. I was just giving us time to work out what we're going to tell them."

"The truth, of course," I replied.

"Sure," Lisa nodded. "But you have to do it the right way. I've got it all worked out."

"I thought you might have," I sighed. "I'm not interested in any more of your stupid ideas."

There's one thing I'll say for Lisa. It's hard to offend her.

"You'll like this one," she said. "You'll like this one a lot."

Chapter 10
Mum and Me

Wendy was waiting on the station platform.

And standing beside her was a policewoman.

"Billie!" Wendy cried, rushing towards me as we stepped off the train, and giving me a big hug.

I waited for the shouting to start but it didn't.

"Thank God you're safe!" she murmured. She hugged me so hard that I thought I might burst. "I've been so scared."

She pulled away and I could see that she had been crying.

"I think, young lady," the policewoman began as we walked towards the car park, "you had better tell us what has been going on."

I took a deep breath but Lisa got there first.

"We're really sorry," she said meekly, "but yesterday, Billie thought she saw her mum."

"Her mum?" Wendy gasped, stopping dead in her tracks. "She doesn't have – I mean, how could she have seen her mother?"

"There was this woman, and she said she was looking for Billie, and then she took her hat off and her hair was red," I gabbled, and then burst into tears.

"We thought she was Billie's real mother," Lisa went on. "That's why we went back to London today. We wanted to find her."

She paused and kicked my ankle. I remembered what she'd told me.

"I kept dreaming about having a proper mother," I gulped. "Someone who would keep me forever and never get rid of me."

Wendy stared at me.

Lisa kicked me again.

"I kept dreaming about my real mum, and the woman on the train looked just like the lady in the dream," I lied.

Lisa had told me that if I talked like this everyone would feel sorry for me and forget to punish me. I held my breath.

"A proper mother?" Wendy sighed. She sounded so upset that I began to feel bad. "And did you find this woman?"

She didn't look at me. She was biting her lip and tapping her foot on the ground.

I nodded.

"She's not my mum, though," I sighed. "She doesn't even have red hair. It was a wig."

"Don't be angry, Wendy," Lisa pleaded. "Billie's been so sad and lonely."

"Right," Wendy said through clenched teeth. "That does it."

My heart sank. She was fed up with me.

Wendy grabbed my hand and marched us both to the car. She opened the door and told us both to get in. After that, the policewoman got into her car and drove off. Wendy took me home and we dropped Lisa off on the way.

The moment Lisa got out of the car Wendy turned to me. "You did a stupid, dangerous and selfish thing today. You do see that, don't you?" she stormed. "I thought someone had kidnapped you, or that you had been run over."

"Sorry," I whispered.

"Why did you do it? Why?" she pleaded.

"Because I want a real mum!" I shouted. "I want to know who my parents are. I want to know if I look like them. I want to belong to someone."

Wendy took a deep breath and turned into the driveway of our house.

"You belong with us, Billie," she said. "We love you. You've always got a home with us."

That's when I said it.

The terrible thing.

"A foster home, you mean," I shouted. "You're not my mum. You're just a foster mum. And that doesn't count!"

****

I heard Wendy crying that night.

And lots of nights after that.

I heard her whispering on the phone.
I saw her filling in forms and muttering to
Steve when they thought I was upstairs
doing homework.

I knew what was happening.

They were planning to send me away.

They'd had enough.

And then one day Wendy came into my
bedroom and asked me a question.

I made her ask it three times because I
thought she was just fooling about.

When I saw that she was dead serious, I
jumped up and down and shouted, "Yes!
Yes!" about 20 times.

That was six months ago.

I'm not Billie Gold any more.

I'm Billie Hunter. I've got a mum called Wendy and a dad called Steve. I've got a gran who lives in Scotland and at half term we went to stay with her.

She called me her lovely wee lassie and put my photo on her bedside table.

You've guessed. The question Wendy asked me was whether I'd let her be my proper mum.

I said "Yes" and Wendy and Steve adopted me.

Wendy said she had wanted to ever since the first time she saw me.

Steve said the only reason they hadn't adopted me ages ago was because they thought my real mum just might turn up.

"We knew she might want to find you, Billie," he told me. "We knew you'd want your real mum and not us if you could choose."

That's where he's wrong. Things have changed.

Like Pixie said, I don't want that sort of real mum any more.

The mum I love – and the one who loves me, and supports me and makes me feel like an important, special person – is right here.

My mum Wendy.

Barrington Stoke would like to thank all its readers for commenting on the manuscript before publication and in particular:

Jill Buckeridge

Grant Burns

J. Cox

Jonny Jones

Harriet Lavis

Scott McNeill

Sabina Moliam

Josh Redmund

Samantha Reilly

Charlene Shaw

Stephen Smith

Become a Consultant!

Would you like to give us feedback on our titles before they are published? Contact us at the address below – we'd love to hear from you!

Barrington Stoke, Sandeman House, Trunk's Close,
55 High Street, Edinburgh EH1 1SR
Tel: 0131 557 2020 Fax: 0131 557 6060
E-mail: info@barringtonstoke.co.uk
Website: www.barringtonstoke.co.uk

If you loved this story, why don't you read . . .

Life Line
by Rosie Rushton
ISBN 1-842990-19-5
£4.99

Have you ever told a fib because it was easier than the truth? Skid finds himself in trouble because he tells one fib too many. But how can he tell the truth about his home life? Cassie is there to help, but who is she?

You can order *Life Line* directly from our website at **www.barringtonstoke.co.uk**

If you loved this story, why don't you read . . .

Angel Dancer

by Frances Mary Hendry

ISBN 1-842991-84-1

£4.99

Ever wanted to dance like an angel?
Brenda's desperate to become a ballerina.
Nothing can stand in her way. Nothing. But
what price will she pay for her one night of
glory?

**You can order *Angel Dancer* directly from our
website at www.barringtonstoke.co.uk**

If you loved this story, why don't you read ...

Letter from America
by Michaela Morgan
ISBN 1-842991-85-X
£4.99

Tommo's fed up. His teacher has had another of her ideas. She wants everyone in the class to have a penpal. Tommo knows it's going to be boring, boring, BORING. But he's in for a big surprise! Share Tommo's sad times and his happy times – and meet Shelley who raps, rhymes and jokes in her letters from America.

You can order *Letter from America* directly from our website at www.barringtonstoke.co.uk